Icy Magic

Anna The Anglerfish Fairy

BY

AANYA GARG

Pharos Books

**Next book
in Icy Magic series**
Sophia the Stonefish fairy

©Publisher

Publisher: Pharos Books (P) Ltd.
Plot No.-55, Main Mother Dairy Road
Pandav Nagar, East Delhi-110092
Phone: 011-40395855, +14049995474
WhatsApp: +91 8368220032
E-mail: sales@pharosbooks.in
Website: www.pharosbooks.in
First Edition: 2022

Printed By: Sushma Book Binding House, Okhla
Industrial Area, Phase II, New Delhi-110020

Anna The Anglerfish Fairy
Aanya Garg

Books in Icy Magic Series

Ocean fairies

Oceana the Ocean fairy

Anna the Anglerfish fairy

Sophia the Stonefish fairy

Olivia the Octopus fairy

Catlyn the Clownfish fairy

Rosella the Rockfish fairy

Molly the Manatee fairy

Dedicated to

My teachers

I appreciate your kindness, patience and all the hard work you put to make learning fun and exciting for me. You helped me become the person I am today. I owe you my lifelong respect.

CONTENTS

Each of the seven ocean fairies has a magical shell to keep the oceans in order. But Fireblast, a squawker, had stolen all the shells to create chaos in the oceans. The ocean fairies' powers are limited in the human world, that is why they took the help of two girls, Alice and Christy, to help them recover the shells. By placing their hands on a fairy when needed, the fairy's power increases. Thus far, only one shell has been found out of seven.

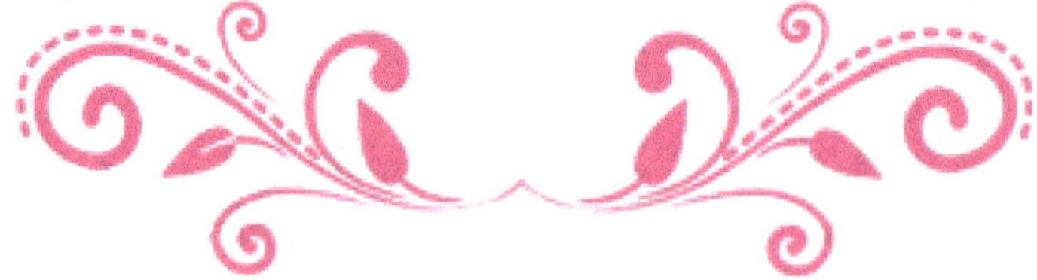

CHAPTER 1

Alice and Christy, who had enrolled in a summer camp organized by Coral Adventures, were playing at the beach. They had just finished their jet ski ride. The kids were given half an hour's free time before their next activity would begin. It was time for beach combing! "Come on!" Alice shouted, "Let's find some shells to put in this bottle and then bury it in the sand."

They kept a sharp eye out for the shell that would fit perfectly in the bottle. Just then, something caught Christy's eye. It was a sparkling, glowing shell. When Christy picked up the shell, she saw Anna the Anglerfish Fairy waving to her from inside the shell.

Anna said, "We need to get to the Icy Palace quickly." Alice and Christy had been waiting to be called to the Icy Palace for their next adventure. Seeing Anna, they understood it was time to find Anna's missing shell. Anna waved her wand and drew an anglerfish in the air. With wings sprouting out of Alice and Christy's back, they flew out of the human world to the Icy Palace.

CHAPTER 2

On reaching Icy Palace, Anna, Alice and Christy met Queen Alexa and King Charles, who greeted them in beautiful voices and led them to the Magic Pond to locate Fireblast. The Magic Pond showed Fireblast sailing on the Atlantic Ocean. In his hand was the topaz shell.

He was using it to cause hurricanes which in turn would put plant, animal and human life in danger.

Anna said sadly, "If he isn't stopped, everything will be ruined. We need to go to the Atlantic Ocean."

With a swirl of her wand, they were sent to the Atlantic Ocean in a flash, sailing in a boat.

They spotted Fireblast sailing in a boat on the ocean. The shell was in his pocket. It was glowing so brightly that they could see its outline through his pants. Christy, Alice and Anna had to think of a plan. They weren't sure if this would work, but they were determined to give it a try. They would try to trick him with a fake sapphire shell.

They sailed their boat towards Fireblast. Christy said to him, "Wouldn't you like to trade this shiny sapphire shell for the topaz shell?" This time Fireblast knew it was a trick. He refused, "I am not taking that sapphire shell unless you give me the real deal. I know you are trying to trick me, just like the last time. But this time I won't fall for it."

CHAPTER 3

Christy and Alice had to think of another plan. Suddenly, an idea popped into Alice's head. She asked Anna, "Since you are an ocean fairy and friends with anglerfish, can you ask your anglerfish to chase Fireblast?" Anna nodded "Yes" and touched her anglerfish-shaped-charm hanging from her necklace and called out to her ocean animal friend, an anglerfish. Immediately an anglerfish leaped out of the water and came close to their boat. It is one of the deadliest fish of the ocean, a round-bodied, dark brown fish with a big

mouth and sharp pointed teeth.

Anna asked the anglerfish if it could try to catch Fireblast. The anglerfish nodded and started to chase him. Fireblast was shocked when he felt his boat tumbling. He knew he was in danger and something was chasing him, but he couldn't see what it was.

Then he saw the anglerfish leaping out of the water. He was terrified to see the scary looking anglerfish. He used his wand to blow off the fish by sending hot winds in its direction. With Alice and Christy holding onto her shoulders, Anna immediately formed a column of thick freezing whirlwind to protect the fish.

The fish sped up the chase. Unable to think of a way to get rid of the anglerfish, he held out the shell from his pocket and called out to the fish, "Eat the shell. I am sure it would taste much better than me." He threw the shell onto the anglerfish's back.

The anglerfish flicked its body and the shell rose up in the air. It caught the shell with its sharp, pointed, needle-like teeth. Then it swam over to the girls and passed the shell to them.

CHAPTER 4

Anna thanked the anglerfish for helping them get their topaz shell from Fireblast. Anglerfish jumped out of the water with a smile, kissed Anna on her cheeks and dived back deep into the water. Alice and Christy waved goodbye to Anglerfish.

Anna touched the shell with her wand and they whizzed away to the Icy Palace to return the topaz shell to the queen. The queen kept it safely in the treasure chest, happy to have the topaz shell back where it belonged.

The Queen and the fairy thanked the girls for once again helping them in recovering the shell from Fireblast and saving the oceans from the chaos. As a token of appreciation, Queen gifted them a sparkly bracelet. Then some fairy dust flew on the girls and they were back on the beach. Everything seemed unchanged there except for the sparkly bracelet on their wrist. Alice and Christy looked at their bracelet with a smile and winked to each other remembering the fairy adventure they just had.

What and where would their next adventure be? How will Alice and Christy help the fairies find the remaining shells? To know, read on in the next book: Sophia the Stonefish Fairy

FUN FACTS

The most remarkable feature that an anglerfish is known for is a fleshy organ that grows from its head and just hangs in front of its mouth. This fleshy organ is actually a piece of its dorsal spine and is called illicium. It is found only in the female. The anglerfish uses it to catch its prey. This organ is shaped like a fishing rod. This is where anglerfish gets its name. Anglers is a common term used for people who enjoy fishing with a rod as a hobby!

At the end of the illicium (fishing rod) is a glowing blob called esca. It serves as a bait to lure the prey. The glow of this esca, or bait, comes from the millions of light-producing bacteria living in it.

Anglerfish are commonly found in Atlantic and Antarctic oceans. The expected life span of an anglerfish is 20 years or more.

The primary hunting technique of an anglerfish is to stay in one spot on the ocean floor to conserve energy. Its illicium attracts fish or crustaceans that are passing by and lures them close to the anglerfish. When prey gets close to its mouth, the anglerfish will strike and consume the meal.

An anglerfish has thin and flexible bones, which allows it to extend its jaw and stomach to an enormous size. Using this ability, it can swallow prey that is twice as large as the body of the anglerfish itself.

An anglerfish can range in length from over three and a half feet to just under one foot long. The biggest anglerfish ever found was more than four feet long.

LABEL THE PARTS?

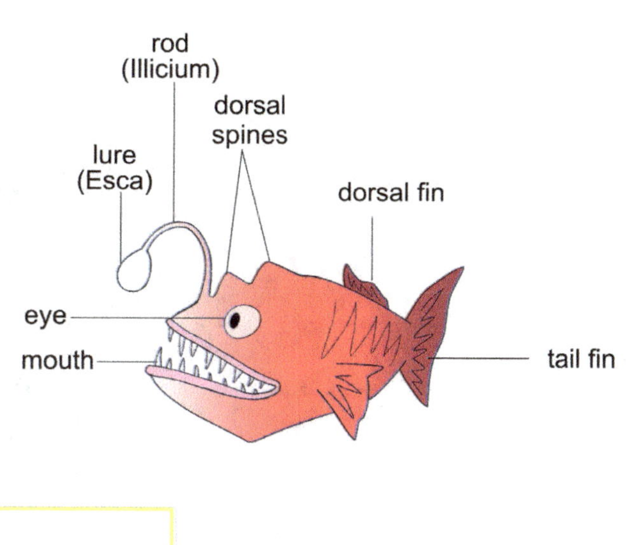

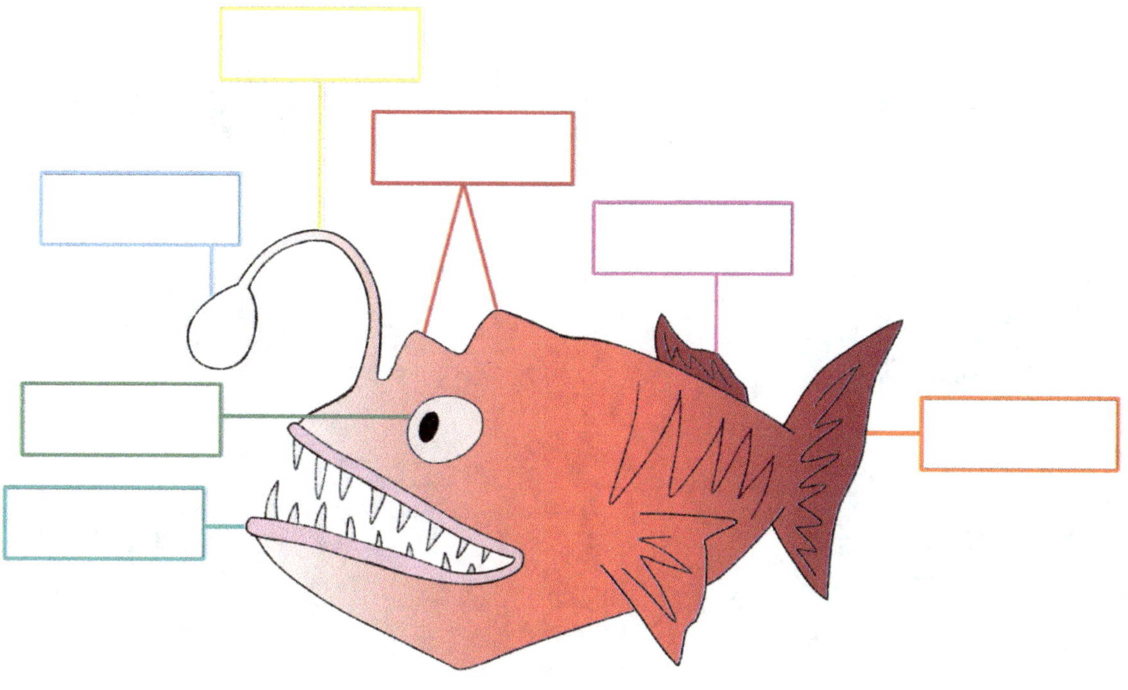

MATCH CORRECTLY

Fairy	Charles
Shell	Atlantic
Ocean	Anglerfish
Animal Friend	Topaz
King	Anna

My special thanks to:

My editor, Li Ping, who edited my books with her usual fine eye to details. Her expertise and advice have been invaluable.

My illustrator, Aru Sharma, who designed my book with patience and panache and rendered the beautiful book cover and page illustrations.

Released Already!

Next book in Icy Magic series
Sophia the Stonefish fairy
Available April 2022